THE MAKING OF

GOODNIGHT MOON

A 50TH ANNIVERSARY RETROSPECTIVE

BY LEONARD S. MARCUS

▄ HARPERTROPHY®

A DIVISION OF HARPERCOLLINSPUBLISHERS

The Making of *Goodnight Moon*: A 50th Anniversary Retrospective
Copyright © 1997 by HarperCollins Publishers
Printed in the U.S.A. All rights reserved.
Typography by Al Cetta
1 2 3 4 5 6 7 8 9 10
❖
First Edition

**India ink study
by Clement Hurd
of the
great green room.**
(Courtesy of Thacher Hurd)

Children, like writers, need rooms of their own, places—whether real or imaginary—of peace and well-being and unconditional love, places where a secure sense of self can begin to grow. That solid sense of being at home in the world is one of the great gifts the adult world has the power to bestow on its children. That is the gift that three generations of children have happily found in the hypnotic, mystery-laden words and joyful pictures of *Goodnight Moon*.

First published in 1947, in the early days of postwar baby boom prosperity, *Goodnight Moon* was a collaboration between Margaret Wise Brown and Clement Hurd, two young and sophisticated creative artists at the height of their powers. Neither Brown nor Hurd had originally planned on a career in children's books. The story of how they met and came to leave such an extraordinary legacy for young children is a many-faceted tale of American art, literature, and popular culture, and of the generation that came of age between the wars.

Born in Brooklyn in 1910 and raised on suburban Long Island, Margaret Wise Brown was the second of three children in a family with deep roots in the American south and midwest. Her father was a prosperous businessman and the son of a former Missouri governor. Her mother had once dreamed of an acting career. Never much of a scholar, young Margaret was an athletic, daydreamy, intuitive child, the neighborhood mischief maker and storyteller. At Hollins College in Virginia, where friends called her Tim (for her golden hair the color of timothy), she rode horses, read Gertrude Stein, and entertained vague notions of becoming a writer.

A few years later, in the fall of 1935, Brown drifted tentatively into the teacher-training program at New York's progressive Bank Street College of Education. Bank Street, which combined one of the nation's first nursery

Margaret Wise Brown in Vinalhaven, Maine.
(Photo by Consuelo Kanaga [1894–1978]. The Brooklyn Museum. Gift of the Estate of Consuelo Kanaga through the Lerner Heller Gallery. Margaret Wise Brown [B. Negative 5 x 2½ inches; 82.65.1824].)

schools with a world-renowned center for the study of early childhood development, stressed learning by doing and had a yeasty, nonconformist atmosphere that proved to be enormously stimulating. It was there that Brown—or Brownie, as she became known—first tried writing stories for young children and found her vocation.

Bank Street's visionary founder, Lucy Sprague Mitchell, had definite ideas about children's learning and literature. She believed that the young start out life fully immersed in the "here and now" world of their home surroundings—the clocks and socks of daily living as revealed to them by their wondrously acute five senses. That being the case, Mitchell said, fairy tales and Mother Goose nonsense—the traditional literature of the nursery—had less to offer small children than might a new "here and now" literature rooted in children's everyday experiences.

Mitchell put her controversial ideas into practice as the author of the widely read *Here and Now Story Book* (1921). Her own writings also inspired experimental works by others (most notably photographer Edward Steichen's

Inspired by his grown daughter's visits
to Bank Street, Edward Steichen created
a highly original picture book for two-year-olds,
featuring photographs of everyday things familiar to
toddlers. Many of the same subjects Steichen chose
for *The First Picture Book* (Harcourt, Brace, 1930)
turn up again in an early color study of objects found
in the great green room.

(Reprinted with permission of Joanna T. Steichen)

First and *Second Picture Book*s of the early 1930s). Mitchell gave encouragement to gifted students like Brownie, and in 1938 she persuaded a Bank Street parent, William R. Scott, to start a publishing company dedicated to the here-and-now idea. Brown became Scott's first editor and most prolific author. Among the artists she met in the course of that exciting work was

Clement Hurd
at his easel in Vermont in the late 1930s.
(Courtesy of Thacher Hurd)

a New York—born painter and muralist, Clement Hurd.

Hurd was a tall, shy, elegant, rail-thin man whose deadpan wit and openness to experimentation delighted Brown from the first. A graduate of St. Paul's and Yale, Hurd had passed up a safe job at his father's bank and sailed for France in 1931 to become an artist. During two exhilarating years abroad, he studied

One of the "Perils of the Sea" murals by Clement Hurd that convinced Margaret Wise Brown that here was a painter capable of illustrating modern books for modern children.
(Courtesy of Thacher Hurd)

painting with Fernand Léger, discovered the vibrant immediacy of flat-painted primary and secondary colors, and developed a boldly simplifed approach to composition and form. When Brown first saw two paintings of Hurd's at a friend's apartment, she thought his "modern" approach perfectly suited to here-and-now-style bookmaking.

The vivid group of artists and writers who gathered around Scott's charismatic editor—Esphyr Slobodkina (*Caps for Sale*), Leonard Weisgard (illustrator of Brown's *The Noisy Book*), Charles G. Shaw (*It Looked Like Spilt Milk*), and Hurd's wife-to-be, Edith Thacher (*Hurry Hurry*)—regarded themselves as a "little Bloomsbury" of young rebels eager to give the boot to Victorian sweetness and sentiment, and to make the picture book new.

Brown and Hurd first collaborated on *Bumble Bugs and Elephants* (1938), an innovative board book that, in a refreshing departure for the time, invited toddlers to create their own stories from simple word patterns and pictures. The following year Hurd captured a bit more of the limelight as the illustrator of Gertrude Stein's first children's book, *The World Is Round*, a freewheeling

There were two little dogs and a great big dog

Double spread from *Bumble Bugs and Elephants* (Scott, 1938).

(Text copyright © by Margaret Wise Brown. Illustration copyright © by Clement Hurd.)

fantasy written by Stein at Brown's prompting. Critics had a field day with the famed expatriate's penchant for repetition ("Gertrude Stein is writing is writing is writing a new Gertrude Stein a new book . . .")

Clement Hurd with his wife, Edith (left),
and Margaret Wise Brown, at the opening
of an exhibition of the artist's work
in New York, 1940. In the background
are sheets of nursery wallpaper based on Hurd's
illustrations for Gertrude Stein's children's book,
The World Is Round (Scott, 1939).

(Photo by Edward Ozern)

William R. Scott, Inc.'s modern books for modern children failed in general to win the approval of the nation's influential librarians, who dismissed the publisher's offerings as faddishly newfangled and subliterary.

Brown relished the controversy. A glamorous, self-dramatizing, fiercely independent woman, she made good sport of demolishing the quaint stereotype of the spinsterly "juveniles" author while writing book after book of unsurpassed poetic lyricism, saucy wit, and emotional honesty.

During a protean fifteen-year-long career during which she wrote over a hundred picture books, Brown worked with a great many illustrators and publishers. But she reserved her most deeply felt manuscripts for Clement Hurd and for Harper & Brothers' fearless young editor (and fellow perfectionist) Ursula Nordstrom.

Brown called her favorite editor Ursula Maelstrom; Nordstrom called *her* Miss Genius. In a career that spanned over thirty years, Nordstrom published tradition-bending books by Ruth Krauss, Crockett Johnson, Maurice Sendak, Louise Fitzhugh, Charlotte Zolotow, John Steptoe, M. E. Kerr, and others. In 1942 she brought out Brown and Hurd's rhapsodic new picture book

**Ursula Nordstrom, director of Harper & Brothers'
Department of Books for Boys and Girls.**

(Courtesy of The Children's Book Council)

The Runaway Bunny. The artist, now married and living in Vermont, had barely time to enjoy the book's critical success (and solid if not quite runaway sales) when the wartime draft called an abrupt temporary halt to his life as an illustrator.

As a child Margaret Wise Brown had adored *Peter Rabbit*, made up her own, scarier versions of "Cinderella" and "Hansel and Gretel," and kept a black cat named Ole King Cole. While Bank Street underscored for her the importance the very young place on everyday things, Brown never doubted the strong affinity that small children also have for make-believe. Wanda Gág's classic *Millions of Cats* (1928), with its beguiling blend of homey immediacy and wild exaggeration, became a touchstone work for her as it also was for Clement Hurd. In *Goodnight Moon* Brown was able to convey, as well as anyone has, a young child's liquid view of the world as a place both near at hand and vast beyond measure, toy bright yet shadow tinged, comfortingly familiar yet at times also fantastically strange.

In one of those apparently effortless creative acts that comes of a lifetime of

preparation, Brown set down the text of *Goodnight Moon* in nearly finished form on awaking one morning in early 1945. The mercurial author who told friends that she "dreamt" her books seems in this instance to have literally done so. She called the new book *Goodnight Room*.

That morning Ursula Nordstrom became the first person to have the

(Facing page) Brown and Hurd both admired Wanda Gág's 1928 classic *Millions of Cats* (left). Rabbit or not, an early study of *Goodnight Moon*'s "old lady whispering hush" (right) bears a striking family resemblance to Gág's "very old woman."

(*Left:* Illustration by Wanda Gág from *Millions of Cats* by Wanda Gág, copyright © 1928 by Coward McCann Inc.; reprinted by permission of Coward McCann Inc.; copyright © renewed by Robert Janssen, 1956. *Right:* Courtesy of the Kerlan Collection.)

Manuscript page from the dummy of *Goodnight Moon* that Brown prepared for Hurd. Brown printed out the text, indicating page breaks; additional notes were by Ursula Nordstrom.

(Courtesy of the Kerlan Collection)

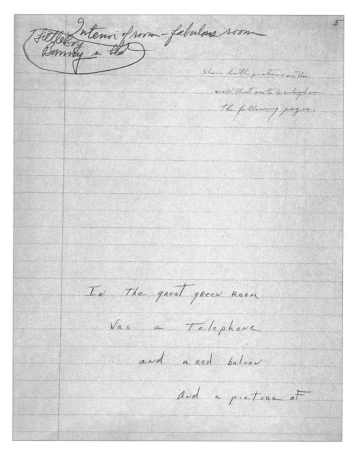

manuscript read aloud to her—over the telephone, by the author herself. Nordstrom, who in later years credited Brown with having taught her all that she knew about picture-book making, accepted the manuscript at once.

In an early typescript Brown experimented with repeating several text lines in the manner of a musical refrain. She also considered—and thought better of—breaking the magical spell of "goodnights" with a silly-sounding, throwaway ending: "Goodnight cucumber/Goodnight fly."

With Clement Hurd not yet back from Pacific wartime service, Nordstrom began contacting other artists about the assignment. At some point, however, Brown seems to have decided that she wanted no one but Hurd for the book. The author who had persuaded Harper to bind another of her books, *Little Fur Family*, in real rabbit's fur, easily got her wish again. When Clement Hurd finally turned up in New York that December, Brown gave him and his wife the use of her Manhattan hideaway, Cobble Court, and in due course sent along her manuscript, with a reproduction of Goya's spirited *Boy in Red* pasted on the cover for inspiration.

Brown, at work in her fanciful
Manhattan hideaway,
Cobble Court, as photographed
by Philippe Halsman
for *Life* magazine. The article ran
in the December 2nd,
1946, issue.

(Photo by Philippe Halsman
copyright © by Halsman Estate)

**Brown and her rambunctious
Kerry blue terrier, Crispian,
as photographed by Halsman.**

(Photo by Philippe Halsman
copyright © by Halsman Estate)

Hurd worked on the illustrations for most of the next year. "The bunny is younger and the old lady is lovable if not 'fairy story,'" he assured Brown and Nordstrom in March. "One reason why I can't get the fairy story feeling is because I don't really like [fairy tales] and think of all the old ladies [in them as] witches."

Confining the action of a picture book to a single room—even the "fabulous room" that Nordstrom told Hurd to devise—was a strikingly original plan. (In 1948, Alfred Hitchcock, with a rather different effect in mind, would attempt a similarly bold exploration of psychological space in his experimental thriller *Rope*.) In the first preliminary layout hashed out by the author, editor, and artist, an identical panoramic view of the room was to be shown in each full-page color spread. It was Hurd's more fluid (and cinematic) idea, however, to subtly vary the field of vision and scale from page to page, thereby gently but firmly guiding the reader through the great green room.

With a baby boom in progress and interest in children's books accordingly on the rise, *Life* commissioned a celebrity profile of Brown, the nation's most

Tempera study by Clement Hurd for *Goodnight Moon* (above). The "old lady" is still a woman; there is a map on the wall and no bookshelf; and the mouse has ventured onto the bunny child's bed. Compare with a later ink study (below)

(Courtesy of the Kerlan Collection)

prolific "Child's Best-Seller." *Life*'s reporter listened in at Harper one day as Hurd's latest paintings got the once-over:

"I like the rabbit. He has real sleepiness."

"Yes, but I'm worried about the yarn; it loses personality and softness."

The author, editor, and artist also worried over the mouse's proximity to the bunny child's bed. Another imaginary mouse, the hero of E. B. White's *Stuart Little*, published by Harper in 1945, had recently made some of the nation's powerful librarian-critics a bit queasy. In one of the great green room's fanciful wall decorations, the udder belonging to the cow that jumped over the moon came under similar scrutiny and for caution's sake was reduced to an anatomical blur.

They argued over whether the "old lady" and child should be depicted as human characters (Hurd's preference) or as rabbits (Brown's and Nordstrom's). Hurd tried the older character both ways. And in one, apparently unique study for the great green room, he introduced the image of a young black boy, modeled possibly on the child who spent the summer of 1946 with him and his wife in rural Connecticut, sponsored by the Fresh Air Fund. Hurd's depiction of a child of color—so unusual for an American picture book of that era—had come out awkwardly. Brown and Nordstrom rightly insisted that Hurd was a better painter of rabbits than of people—and so rabbits it was. And with a wink and a nod, a framed map of the Americas was replaced by a scene from *The Runaway Bunny*.

In postwar America, returning veterans were finding work, starting families, and moving to the suburbs by the millions. A vastly expanded market for children's books was one of the consequences of this massive social change. During the 1947 holiday season the new twenty-five-cent Golden Books, sold off racks at supermarkets, proved their appeal to economy-minded parents. For those with a little more to spend, the tried-and-true classics made dependable gifts, as did the latest titles by favorite living authors like Wanda Gág, H. A. Rey, Dr. Seuss, and Margaret Wise Brown.

    Goodnight Moon was one of three Brown picture books published by Harper that fall. (The others were *The First Story*, illustrated by Marc Simont, and *The*

One of several preliminary designs for the cover of *Goodnight Moon*.
(Courtesy of the Kerlan Collection)

Sleepy Little Lion, with photographs by Ylla.) It appeared to strong reviews and enjoyed a robust initial sale of more than 6,000 copies.

Not everyone liked the book. The New York Public Library's Anne Carroll Moore, who had reacted strongly against Bank Street's efforts to grow literature in the laboratory of modern social science, pointedly declined to place

Goodnight Moon on the library's prestigious annual list of recommended titles.

Over the next few years, sales slackened off predictably as newer titles (including a breathtaking thirty-two picture books by Brown herself) moved to the fore. What happened next, however—an unanticipated surge in sales in 1953, followed up by a nearly uninterrupted increase in annual demand ever since—was to become the stuff of publishing legend. No one knows for sure why it happened. Parents over the years seem to have discovered the book and told their friends about it, again and again.

Although widely appreciated in her lifetime, Brown did not live to see this ultimate vindication of her boldly innovative art. Vacationing in France in November of 1952, she died of an embolism following routine surgery. Doctors at a more modern hospital of the time might easily have saved her. She was forty-two years old.

Clement Hurd lived on into his eighties, painting, teaching, and illustrating over seventy children's books, including more than forty written by his wife, Edith Thacher Hurd. In later years, people meeting the accomplished couple

Clement Hurd in the late 1970s.
(Courtesy of Thacher Hurd)

"'Goodnight room. Goodnight moon.'"

New Yorker cartoon by James Stevenson, January 8, 1990.

(Drawing by James Stevenson: Copyright © 1990 The New Yorker Magazine, Inc.)

(Facing page, left) *New Yorker* cartoon by Bruce Eric Kaplan,
June 24/July 1, 1996.

(Drawing by Bruce Eric Kaplan: Copyright © 1996 The New Yorker Magazine, Inc.)

(Facing page, right) Cover from *Boom Baby Moon* by Sean Kelly,
illustrated by Ron Hauge (Dell, 1993).

(From *Boom Baby Moon* by Sean Kelly. Copyright © 1993 by Sean Kelly.
Used by permission of Dell Books, a division of Bantam Doubleday Dell Publishing Group, Inc.)

often casually assumed that *Goodnight Moon* must be among their collaborations, too. With many another fine book to her credit, Edith naturally bristled at the error. "Living with *Goodnight Moon*" was her title for a memoir that, in wry but rueful moments, she thought about writing.

By 1956 Ursula Nordstrom was contemplating a *Goodnight Moon* washable cloth edition, noting in a letter to the artist that "children young enough to love that book do tear the pages." Nothing came of the idea, the notion of books made just for babies still being a comparatively new and suspect one at mid century, baby boom or not. When a board-book edition finally appeared

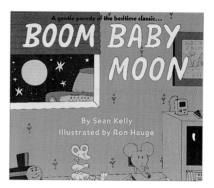

"Call me shallow—I *like* 'Goodnight Moon.' "

in 1991, things came full circle at last, for it was the proven success of *Goodnight Moon*, more than that of any other book of the postwar decades, that confirmed for parents and publishers alike the need for books specially designed for the youngest ages.

As copies of *Goodnight Moon* found their way into ever more homes and libraries, the book sailed headlong into the nation's cultural mainstream.

Mention of the great green room became a flash point of shared experience for the television viewers of *Maude* and *Murphy Brown*. In February 1988 word of Clement Hurd's death prompted a *New York Times* editorial and a poignant television tribute from *CBS News Sunday Morning*'s Charles Kuralt.

By the 1990s *Goodnight Moon* had become all but synonymous in pop cultural shorthand with kids' bedtime books and rituals. It had also been discovered as a convenient springboard for the observations of columnists, cartoonists, and parodists with something to say about the chances for a happy childhood, or a good night's rest, in late-twentieth-century America.

Amid all the commotion, Brown and Hurd's remarkable little book went on offering "readers who fear the dark," as *The New York Times* had said, "a world that is warm and safe and inviting." And on reconsideration the New York Public Library now honored *Goodnight Moon* as one of its "Books of the Century," noting in its 1996 centennial exhibition catalogue that "few books," whether intended for children or adults, "have been as cherished."

Among the fan letters that Clement Hurd received over the years was one from the mother of a nineteen-month-old who had been asking for *Goodnight Moon* every night for the past week or so. The previous evening, as his mother watched, the child pressed his right foot down onto one of the pictures of the great green room, saying "Walk! Walk!" He then tried his left foot. Then he burst into tears. The child had wanted to climb inside the great green room, a place as real for him as it also was magical.

Be glad for that child—and for *any* child lucky enough, as Margaret Wise Brown once said, to be "lift[ed] . . . for a few minutes from his own problems of shoelaces that won't tie and busy parents and mysterious clock-time . . . [into] the timeless world of story."

Clement Hurd visiting Margaret Wise Brown at her summer house in Vinalhaven, Maine.
(Courtesy of Thacher Hurd)

BIBLIOGRAPHY OF GOODNIGHT MOON

1947	First American edition (Harper & Brothers)
1975	First British edition (World's Work)
1977	First American paperback edition (Harper Trophy)
1979	First Japanese edition (Hyoronsha)
1981	First French edition (L'Ecole de Loisirs)
1983	First Hebrew edition (adam motsi imha-or)
	First Swedish edition (Carlsen)
1984	*Goodnight Moon Room: A Pop-Up Book* (Harper & Row)
1986	First Spanish edition (SITESA)
1991	First American board-book edition (HarperCollins)
1995	Second Spanish edition (Harper Arco Iris)
1996	First Korean edition (Sigong-sa)